WANTED:
Marko Khen,
interplanetary pirate.

CRIME:
Kidnapping. Mutation.

WHEREABOUTS:
Unknown.

YOUR MISSION:
Find Marko Khen and bring back
the rare animals he has stolen and
turned into monsters.

**Bantam Books in the
Be An Interplanetary Spy** Series

#1 **FIND THE KIRILLIAN!**
by Seth McEvoy
illustrated by Marc Hempel
and Mark Wheatley

#2 **THE GALACTIC PIRATE**
by Seth McEvoy
illustrated by Marc Hempel
and Mark Wheatley

BE AN INTERPLANETARY SPY

2

The Galactic Pirate

by Seth McEvoy
illustrated by Marc Hempel
and Mark Wheatley

A Byron Preiss Book

BANTAM BOOKS
TORONTO · NEW YORK · LONDON · SYDNEY

Seth McEvoy, author, is an active member of the *Science Fiction Writers of America*; a video game designer and programmer; and is currently writing a critical study of the work of Samuel R. Delany.

Marc Hempel and *Mark Wheatley*, illustrators, joined forces in 1980 as Insight Studios to produce comics, illustrations, and graphic design. Marc Hempel has a degree in Painting and Illustration from Northern Illinois University. His work has appeared in *Heavy Metal*, *Epic Illustrated*, *Bop*, *Fantastic Films*, *Video Action*, and *Eclipse*. Mark Wheatley has a degree in Communication Arts and Design from Virginia Commonwealth University. His work has appeared in *Metal*, *Epic Illustrated*, Zebra Books and on Avalon Hill Games. Currently he and Marc are collaborating on a graphic story series, *Mars*.

RL3, IL age 9 and up

THE GALACTIC PIRATE
A Bantam Book/June 1983

Special thanks to Judy Gitenstein, Laure Smith, Ron Buehl, Anne Greenberg, Ellen Steiber, Lucy Salvino, Laura Dirksen, John Pierard, Rick Brightfield, Carol Wheatley and Ron Bell.

Cover art and book design by Marc Hempel Mechanical Production by Insight Studios

Typesetting by Graphic/Data Services

"BE AN INTERPLANETARY SPY" is a trademark of Byron Preiss Visual Publications, Inc.

ISBN 0-553-23507-9

Published simultaneously in the United States and Canada

PRINTED IN THE UNITED STATES OF AMERICA

O   0 9 8 7 6 5 4 3

Introduction

You are an Interplanetary Spy. You are about to embark on a dangerous mission. On your mission you will face challenges that may result in your death.

You work for the Interplanetary Spy Center, a far-reaching organization devoted to stopping crime and terrorism in the galaxy. While you are on your mission, you will take your orders from the Interplanetary Spy Center. Follow your instructions carefully.

You will be traveling alone on your mission. If you are captured, the Interplanetary Spy Center will not be able to help you. Only your wits and your sharp spy skills will help you reach your goal. Be careful. Keep your eyes open at all times.

If you are ready to meet the challenge of being an Interplanetary Spy, **turn to Page 1.**

You are an Interplanetary Spy. You have just boarded your starship and are awaiting orders from the Spy Center. To receive the information about your mission, enter your Interplanetary Spy ISBN code number below:

Check the back cover of this book for your Interplanetary Spy ISBN code number. **Turn to page 2.**

A small band of criminals has been stealing rare animals from several planets in Space Sector 17. Using an illegal mutation ray, they change the stolen animals into monsters.

These monsters are then used to terrorize and steal from innocent worlds. The most recent thefts have been from the Interplanetary Zoo.

Before: Normal Rantrog

After:
Mutated Rantrog

The stolen animals are among the most precious and rare animals in the star system.

Turn to page 3 for more information.

The band of criminals works for Marko Khen, the Galactic Pirate. He is extremely dangerous and an expert in robotics, the science of robots. Beware of his robot bird!

Prince Quizon

The robot bird was last seen near the Towers of Alvare, just before they were destroyed by two mutant monsters. Prince Quizon of Alvare fears that Marko Khen will attack again soon.

Turn to page 29.

Your sound scan showed a Kasanga code coming from the submarine.

As you fly toward the submarine, it fires at you!

Your biodroid ducks the blast and plunges into the water to follow the submarine. The 'droid can swim as fast as he can fly!

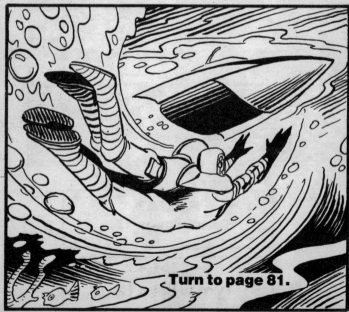

Turn to page 81.

The pouch from Interplanetary Spy Center arrives. But it has *two* artificial hands inside. You must pick the correct hand quickly before the med-ray wears off. If you do not know which hand is the Klagon Hand, consult page 33.

A   **B**

Hand A?
Turn to page 15.

Hand B?
Turn to page 12.

6 Your path is blocked by steel bars coming up through the ground. You try to squeeze between the bars, but the bars are moving.

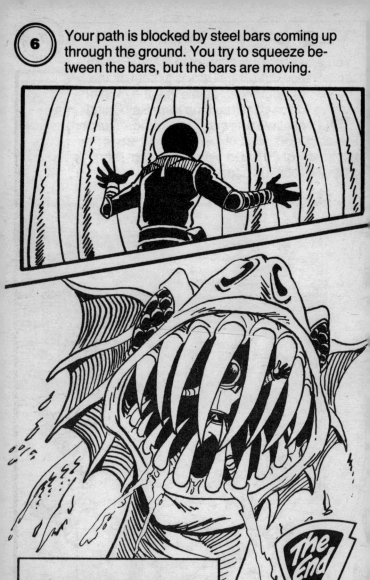

Wait! They aren't bars at all. They are the teeth of a burrowing Jawsnatcher!

The End

ヿ＝ｱＤ≡ｒ = DANGER

You press the button marked DANGER. An emergency cut-off wall starts to seal off the control area, but you realize that the mutant Marko will be drowned if he remains behind it. Your mission is to bring Marko Khen back alive. You must save the Galactic Pirate!

Turn to page 14.

Prince Quizon of Alvare was able to identify one of the monsters. It was a mutated Kasanga, a rare animal that lived in the Interplanetary Zoo before being captured by Marko Khen's agents.

Prince Quizon identified it by tracing its computer ID code. Use your wrist scanner to identify a Kasanga computer ID code. It is the only one that appears once.

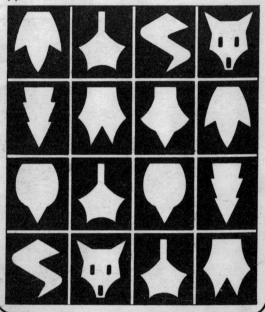

Kasanga computer ID code?
Turn to page 13.

Kasanga computer ID code?
Turn to page 26.

Warning! Warning! Warning! Your ship is drifting into a dangerous asteroid belt! You see two rescue stations in the distance. Your computer tells you that you only have three bursts of fuel remaining. Which station can be reached by only three straight lines?

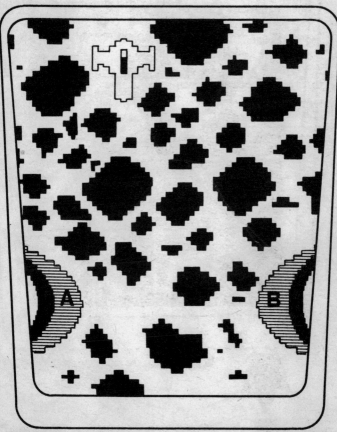

Station A?
Turn to page 32.

Station B?
Turn to page 28.

Excellent piloting! You fly into the correctly shaped dock and land your starship easily.

8

Kasangas are peaceful plant eaters, which live in the zoo's grasslands. You must make your way through the maze of indoor cages until you come to the grassland zone.

You get out and begin searching for the area in which the Kasangas are kept. The center of the zoo is a maze of indoor cages, while the outer parts are divided into different zones, including grassland and forest.

Enter

Turn to page 6.

Turn to page 91.

You made a fatal mistake. Everything blows up! Your next of kin will be notified of your heroism.

12

Sorry! You picked a Mekron Hand, which is for *right* hands only. Your *left* hand was prepared by the med-ray because Klagon Hands are *left* hands. The med-ray has already worn off. You request permission from Spy Center to go ahead with the mission anyway. You assure them that your laser is good enough for you.

PERMISSION GRANTED!

As you take off, you get this order from Spy Center: Investigate the remaining Kasangas housed in the Interplanetary Zoo.

The Interplanetary Zoo is currently orbiting around the planet Frandor in Sector 5. You set your course for Sector 5 and blast off.

Turn to page 27.

This is not a Kasanga computer ID code.

It belongs to a Grax! For this mission you must be able to identify the computer ID codes of animals so that you can recognize the stolen animals, no matter what their forms are. Try again:

Computer ID codes resemble part of an animal's body. Look at the Kasanga's foot. Then compare it with the code shapes below.

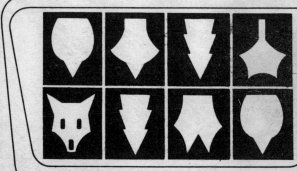

Kasanga computer ID code? Turn to page 26.

Kasanga computer ID code? Turn to page 37.

You tell your biodroid to go through an exit hatch. He grabs an oxygen tank from the wall. Then he goes out into the water. He swims through the hole in the portal and into the control room.

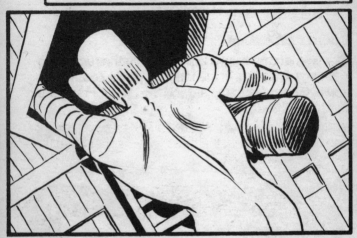

You watch him reach Marko, who is unconscious and drowning. His electrical powers are gone. Your 'droid puts an oxygen mask over Marko's face just in time.

Turn to page 101.

Good! You fit the Klagon Hand over your *left* hand, which the med-ray has prepared. A code word lights up on your computer screen:

> DOMINO

It is your code name for this mission.

Spy Center orders you to investigate the remaining Kasangas housed in the Interplanetary Zoo. The zoo is currently in orbit around the planet Frandor in Sector 5.

You must set your starship's course for Frandor. To do so, you must pick the three buttons that have the same type of pattern.

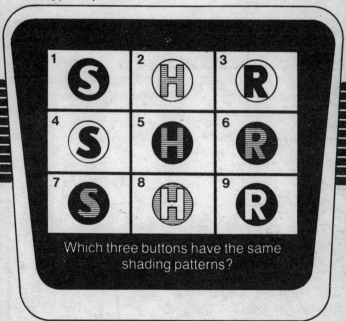

Which three buttons have the same shading patterns?

1-8-9? Turn to page 9.

7-5-6? Turn to page 59.

16

You turn to see who blasted you, but you don't see anyone! Your attacker must be invisible.

You must use your Klagon Hand to make your attacker visible. You release a proton ray, which covers your attacker with microdots. You must darken only the triangles to see your attacker. Do not darken any of the diamonds!

Do you see a lion? Turn to page 23.

Do you see a cobra? Turn to page 30.

Inside the factory, you find hundreds of biodroids "growing" in nutrient tanks. There are many kinds of biodroids for different tasks.

You must go through the maze of nutrient tanks in the factory until you reach the pattern that is similar to the artificial skin (see page 31). Careful! Some of the tanks may explode if they are scanned.

● = Tank

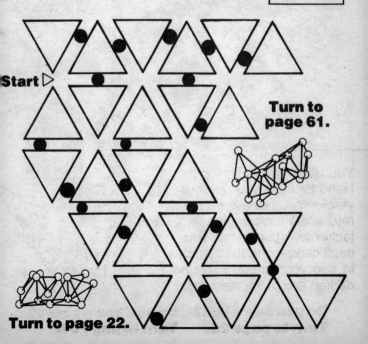

Start ▷

Turn to page 61.

Turn to page 22.

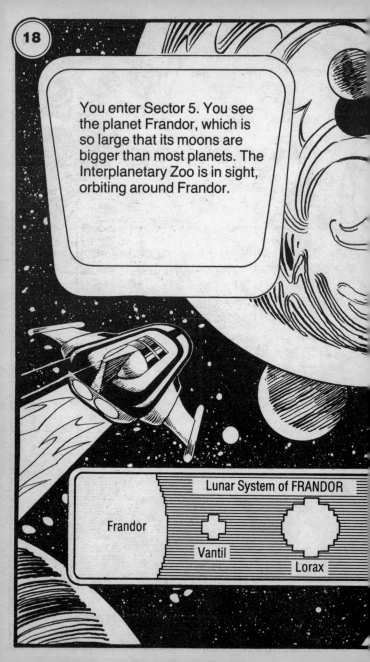

You enter Sector 5. You see the planet Frandor, which is so large that its moons are bigger than most planets. The Interplanetary Zoo is in sight, orbiting around Frandor.

Lunar System of FRANDOR

Frandor

Vantil

Lorax

Your computer shows you the Frandor system. The Interplanetary Zoo is between Aquist and Lorax.

Aquist Zeta Quondam Pakhee

Turn to page 24.

The Klagon Hand is being sent to you by an Interplanetary Spy Center pouch. While you wait for it, you must prepare your hand to accept the Klagon Hand.

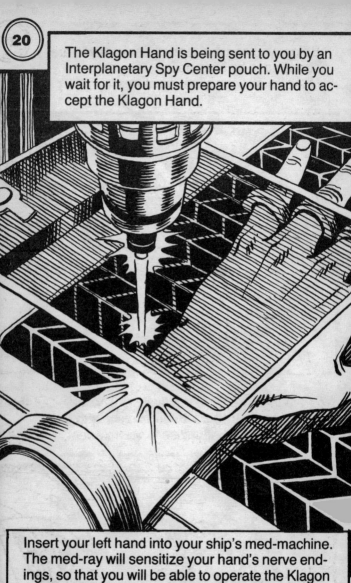

Insert your left hand into your ship's med-machine. The med-ray will sensitize your hand's nerve endings, so that you will be able to operate the Klagon Hand as if it were your own!

Turn to page 5.

Before you can make another move you are surrounded by alien police. They are Nishells, strange silent creatures.

You tell them your code name is DOMINO. But the Nishells are deaf! You try to explain with sign language, but Nishell justice is not only deaf, it is blind.

The End

Before you can find out any more you are grabbed by biodroid sentries. They think you are a runaway biodroid!

You struggle to escape, but they take you to a nutrient tank. You resist, but the liquid in the tank makes you sleepy. The biodroids attach nerve bundles to your skin.

If you fall asleep, you will be under their control. Unfortunately, you aren't able to stay awake forever.

The End

You think you see a lion. You shoot a laser beam from your Klagon Hand, aiming at the center.

23

But it isn't a lion. A glistening, metallic cobra unfolds its coils. Your shot misses, and the cobra crushes you in its coils before you can fire again. You also see Marko Khen's robot bird, reporting back your failure!

The End

You fly your ship toward the narrow landing platform of the Interplanetary Zoo.

The landing platform has docking slots for different starships. Which slot exactly fits your ship? Decide carefully. You must radio ahead to reserve an odd- or even-numbered dock.

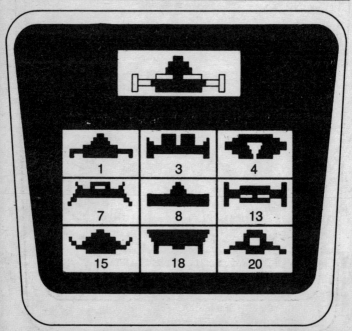

An even-numbered dock? Turn to page 10.
An odd-numbered dock? Turn to page 75.

You get back to your ship and blast off for Zeta. Your immediate goal is to find a link to Marko Khen. The biodroid factory might give you the clue you need.

Danger! Asteroids dead ahead!

If your ship stays on its present course, will it hit the stationary asteroids? The arrow points in the direction your ship will go. Change your course if you think there will be a collision. Otherwise, don't waste fuel!

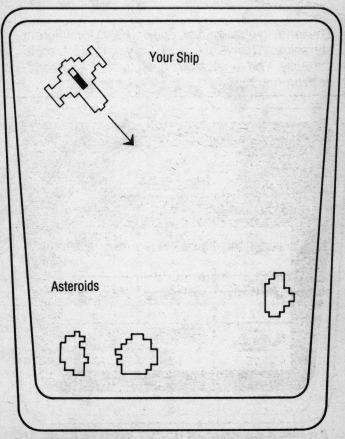

Your Ship

Asteroids

Miss?
Turn to page 28.

Hit?
Turn to page 116.

Good! You have identified
the computer ID code
of the Kasanga.

This is what the normal adult male Kasanga looks
like. Compare it with the picture on page 3. They look
very different, but the computer ID codes are the
same!

Here are the codes from the animals that
were recently stolen from the Interplanetary
Zoo. Study them carefully.

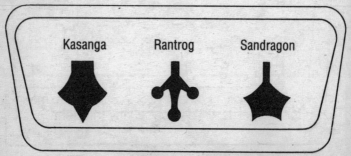

Kasanga   Rantrog   Sandragon

Turn to page 33.

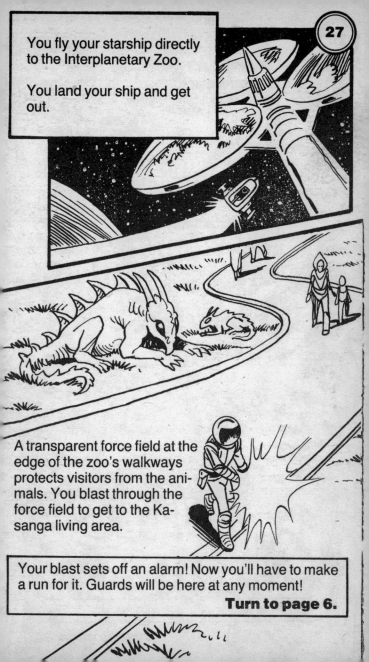

You fly your starship directly to the Interplanetary Zoo.

You land your ship and get out.

A transparent force field at the edge of the zoo's walkways protects visitors from the animals. You blast through the force field to get to the Kasanga living area.

Your blast sets off an alarm! Now you'll have to make a run for it. Guards will be here at any moment!

Turn to page 6.

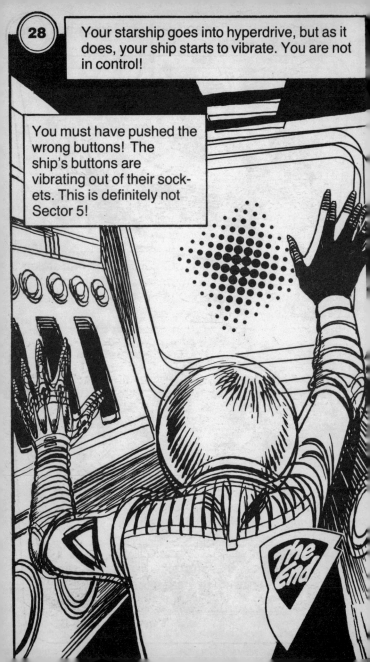

Your mission is to find and capture Marko Khen and his criminal agents.

You must also rescue the animals that he has stolen and, if mutated, change them back to their normal forms. None of the animals should be endangered because they are extremely rare.

Turn to page 8.

You see a glistening robot cobra. You shoot it with your freeze ray, covering it with a spray of ice.

You also see Marko Khen's robot bird, but it flies away before you can blast it!

You approach the cobra, but it blows up when your scan ray touches it!

Marko Khen knows you are after him. You must move even more swiftly now! **Turn to page 25.**

You examine the wounded Kasanga. You find traces of something under one of its claws. It might be proof of an attack by Marko Khen's agents! You put a sample in your pocket analyzer.

You find skin under the Kasanga's claw. Is it human skin or artificial skin? This front view of its molecular structure is what you see:

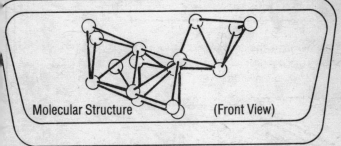

Molecular Structure　　　　　(Front View)

Which of the two side views below is the same as the front view?

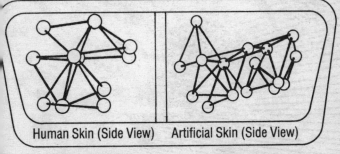

Human Skin (Side View)　　Artificial Skin (Side View)

**This one?
Turn to page 58.**　　　**This one?
Turn to page 77.**

You navigate through the asteroids carefully, but something seems to be pulling you off your course!

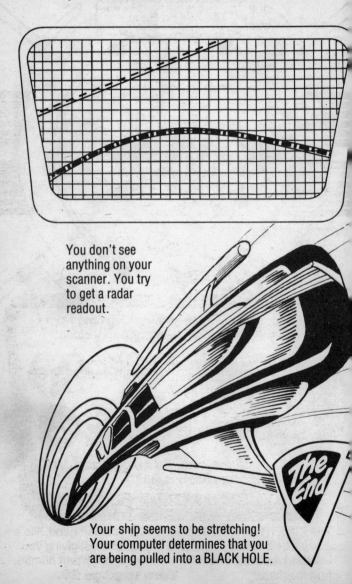

You don't see anything on your scanner. You try to get a radar readout.

The End

Your ship seems to be stretching! Your computer determines that you are being pulled into a BLACK HOLE.

This mission may bring you face-to-face with unexpected dangers. Interplanetary Spy Center will provide you with a special weapon to use in life-and-death situations:

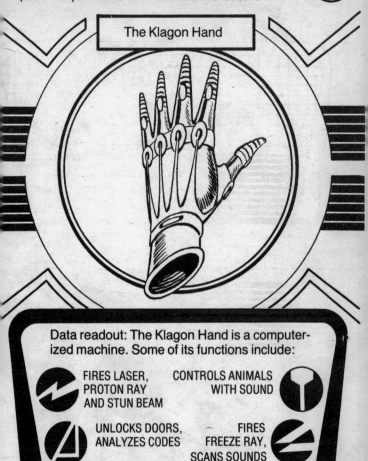

The Klagon Hand

Data readout: The Klagon Hand is a computer-ized machine. Some of its functions include:

FIRES LASER, PROTON RAY AND STUN BEAM

CONTROLS ANIMALS WITH SOUND

UNLOCKS DOORS, ANALYZES CODES

FIRES FREEZE RAY, SCANS SOUNDS

Caution: If you use the Hand at close range, the blast will bounce back at you.

The Klagon Hand will be placed over your left hand, like a glove. But it will be connected to your nerves, giving you lightning reflexes. You will become a cyborg: part human, part machine. **Turn to page 20.**

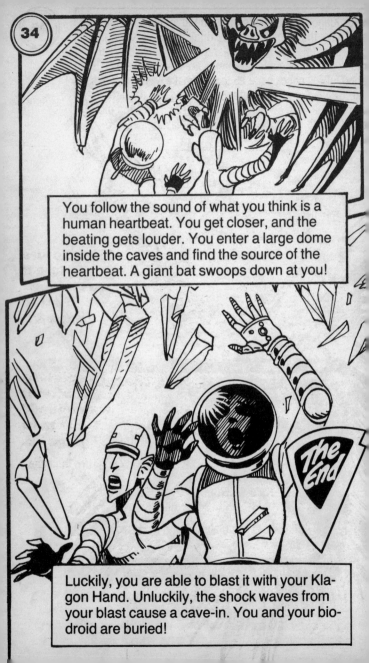

34

You follow the sound of what you think is a human heartbeat. You get closer, and the beating gets louder. You enter a large dome inside the caves and find the source of the heartbeat. A giant bat swoops down at you!

The End

Luckily, you are able to blast it with your Klagon Hand. Unluckily, the shock waves from your blast cause a cave-in. You and your bio-droid are buried!

Your Klagon Hand blasts through the force field. You approach the animals that you think might be Kasangas. Careful! They may be Marapangs, which look very much like Kasangas! Marapangs are deadly meat eaters. Quickly check page 26 to see what a Kasanga looks like. Study the picture below. Then fold this page toward you on the dotted line. You will see a second picture formed. Which picture shows a Kasanga? Go toward that animal!

The picture before it was folded? Turn to page 87.

The picture after it was folded? Turn to page 36.

(Turn the page.)

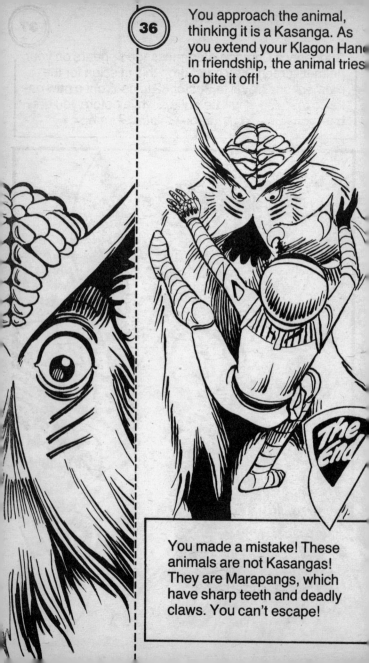

36

You approach the animal, thinking it is a Kasanga. As you extend your Klagon Hand in friendship, the animal tries to bite it off!

You made a mistake! These animals are not Kasangas! They are Marapangs, which have sharp teeth and deadly claws. You can't escape!

Suddenly a Crimson Alert message appears on your helmet screen. You must drop this mission for the moment and travel to Sector 82 to confront a new galactic menace. It will be quite a while before you get back to your search for the Galactic Pirate.

You and your biodroid must act now. At the count of three, you both fire at Marko Khen. You use the Klagon Hand's laser, and your biodroid uses his eye beam.

The combined rays shove Marko into the mutation chamber! The door slams behind him. The Galactic Pirate is knocked out. Before you can celebrate, you hear an odd beeping sound above you.

WIR BLEEP WIR BLEEP WIR BLEEP

Turn to page 109.

You and your biodroid go through the door marked = 7 ··· 8 = ~.

You come face-to-face with one of Marko's mutant monsters! You are too close to blast it with your Hand. The door automatically closes behind you. Guess who's hungry!

The End

You try to grasp the ship with your Klagon Hand. But the illusion ray makes you pick a shape that isn't there! You grab empty air!

You plunge downward. The illusion ray stops just in time for you to see the volcanic moon Lorax. Too late. You are about to become Interplanetary Stew!

The End

A ferocious Makpan flies out at you! You are much too close for your Hand to be of any use. You were looking for rare animals but not one like this. Get ready to be an Interplanetary Lunch!

The End

42

The Cranex is too big to blast with your Klagon Hand. You and the 'droid must get past it and catch up with Marko's submarine.

You can neutralize the tendrils by blasting the tips with your stun ray in a series of straight lines. How many lines will it take to connect the tendril tips?

11 lines?
Turn to
page 89.

9 lines?
Turn to
page 92.

You and your biodroid look down the tunnel where Marko Khen vanished.

You must follow him, but the tunnel twists and turns in different directions.

Note: You can go under a line.

This way?
Turn to page 100.

This way?
Turn to
page 113.

You pushed the wrong button! Fire races through Marko's submarine. As the flames engulf you, there is no time to get out!

The End

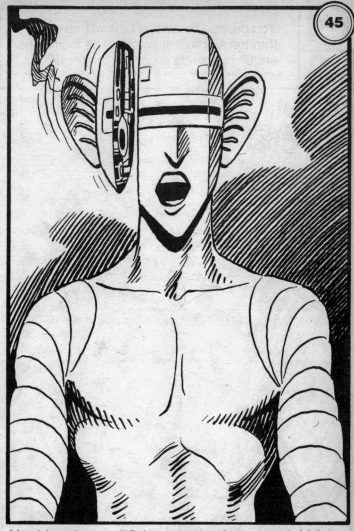

You blast the small flying creature, but you only hit its wing. The creature hovers next to your biodroid. *Wait!* Now you know why it seems familiar! The creature looks like it came from the side of your biodroid's head! You didn't hit the creature's wing, you hit its ear!

Turn to page 46.

The creature attaches itself to the flat side of your bio-droid's head! It must have split off earlier, but how could it go off on its own?

Suddenly, your biodroid changes his expression. Something is wrong! His visor opens and, for the first time, you can see the 'droid's eyes. You don't like the look on the biodroid's face.

Turn to page 47.

"I am under the control of Marko Khen," the 'droid says.

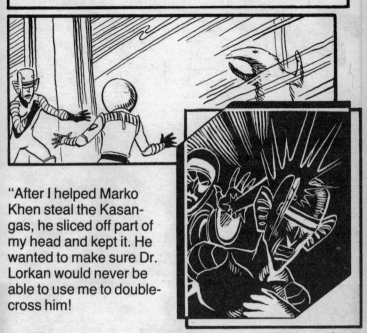

"After I helped Marko Khen steal the Kasan-gas, he sliced off part of my head and kept it. He wanted to make sure Dr. Lorkan would never be able to use me to double-cross him!

"The smaller part of my head can control the rest of me," the biodroid continues. "It is now in charge. It wants me to destroy the Klagon Hand!"

Turn to page 48.

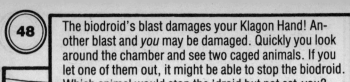

48 The biodroid's blast damages your Klagon Hand! Another blast and *you* may be damaged. Quickly you look around the chamber and see two caged animals. If you let one of them out, it might be able to stop the biodroid. Which animal would stop the 'droid but not eat you?

Tooth Pattern

Tooth Pattern

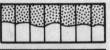

Claw Pattern

Claw Pattern

Free this animal? Turn to page 50.

Free this animal? Turn to page 107.

You goofed, Interplanetary Spy! Everything explodes! The blast triggers off a space-time warp. You are transported ahead in space and time.

When you wake up, you find yourself on the way to page 63.

49

But you don't quite make it.

The End

You free the animal. With its flat teeth and limbs, it is not a meat eater. But the biodroid doesn't know that it also isn't a biodroid eater, and so it fires at the animal. The blast bounces harmlessly off the animal's thick hide. The animal trumpets in rage and picks the biodroid up in its trunk!

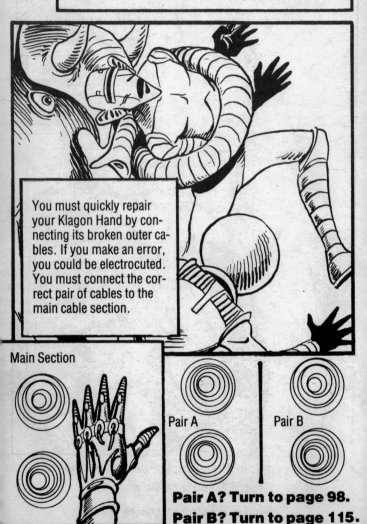

You must quickly repair your Klagon Hand by connecting its broken outer cables. If you make an error, you could be electrocuted. You must connect the correct pair of cables to the main cable section.

Main Section

Pair A

Pair B

Pair A? Turn to page 98.
Pair B? Turn to page 115.

You stun Larat Roz with a right-angle shot from your Klagon Hand!

You search his unconscious body and find a computer circuit card.

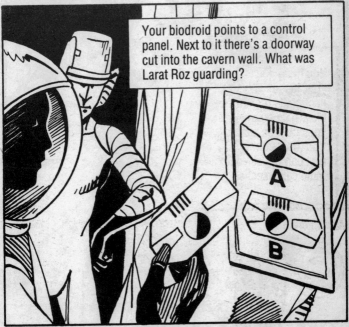

Your biodroid points to a control panel. Next to it there's a doorway cut into the cavern wall. What was Larat Roz guarding?

A

B

Plug the card into the correct panel slot to find out.

Slot A? Turn to page 112.

Slot B? Turn to page 41.

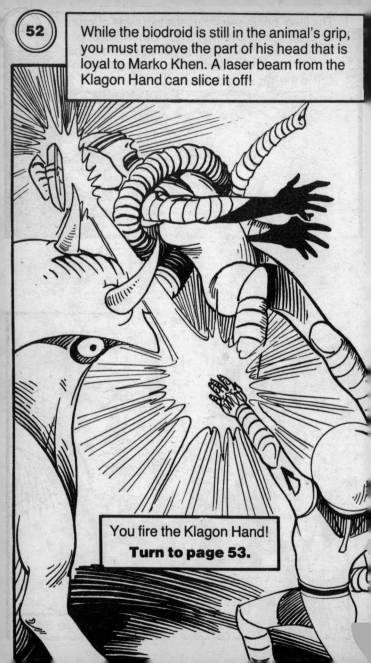

52

While the biodroid is still in the animal's grip, you must remove the part of his head that is loyal to Marko Khen. A laser beam from the Klagon Hand can slice it off!

You fire the Klagon Hand!
Turn to page 53.

The laser beam separates the two parts of your biodroid's head perfectly. Before the smaller part can get away, you freeze it with a blast from your Klagon Hand. The ice will stop it from attaching itself to the 'droid again.

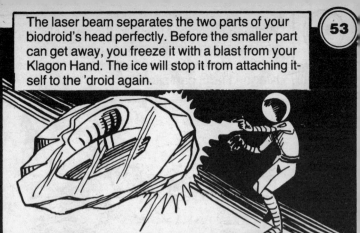

You calm the animal who saved you by speaking your code name, DOMINO, into your Klagon Hand. The creature gently drops the biodroid. He is on your side again, and he sees something behind you!

Turn to page 54.

54 Even encased by ice, the other part of the 'droid is still under Marko Khen's control. It flies to the mutation chamber and turns it on! Then the little 'droid crashes.

The Galactic Pirate wakes up as the mutation ray turns him and the stolen animal into mutant monsters! The mutant Marko Khen is charged with high-voltage electricity. They smash their way out of the chamber with ease. **Turn to page 97.**

Turn to page 97.

You and your biodroid must find Larat Roz before he finds you! Using your Klagon Hand, you try to track the sound of Larat Roz's heartbeat.

The Hand picks up several cave sounds: a river, the wind, animals, and heartbeats! There are two kinds of heartbeats, alien and human, shown below. Which one is your Klagon Hand picking up? You must head in that direction.

Alien Heartbeat

Human Heartbeat

Turn to page 93.

Turn to page 34.

56

As you break through the window a piece of the glass punctures Dr. Lorkan's suit. She gasps for breath.

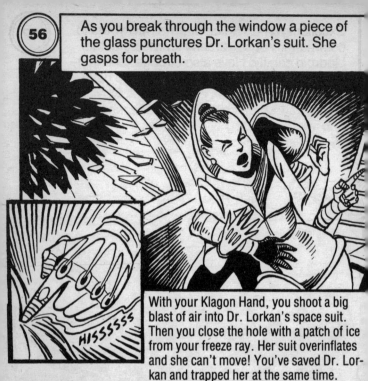

With your Klagon Hand, you shoot a big blast of air into Dr. Lorkan's space suit. Then you close the hole with a patch of ice from your freeze ray. Her suit overinflates and she can't move! You've saved Dr. Lorkan and trapped her at the same time.

Turn to page 111.

Excellent work! The biodroid is now yours to command. You've already learned that this biodroid can fly. He is also stronger and faster than most 'droids, and he seems to have other abilities you don't know about. Obviously, Dr. Lorkan changed him after she got him from the factory.

You find notes about a mutation ray, one that could do just what Marko Khen does— mutate animals!

Your wrist scanner sounds an alarm. Someone is attacking your starship!

Ship Alert!
Warning!
Warning!
Warning!

Turn to page 110.

58

You decide it is human flesh. If it had been artificial flesh, you might have been able to trace it to the factory where it was made.

You look for further clues, but you find nothing. You radio Spy Center to see if any new data has come in.

Data file: An unusual number of starships has been lost near the planet Doorna. Piracy suspected.

Marko Khen is the most infamous space pirate in the galaxy. He may be behind the lost starships as well as the animal theft. You take off for Doorna. But when you get there, a strange ray blasts your ship. Out of control, you spiral down to the planet below. Your ship crashes!

The End

You fired the correct buttons.

7-5-6 SPACE SECTOR SET

S	H	R
SET BOOST	HYPERDRIVE SET	ROCKETS SET

You are now on course for Sector 5. Your starship goes into hyperdrive and quickly transports you to the planet Frandor.

Turn to page 18.

You whisper your code name, DOMINO, into the Klagon Hand. It converts your voice into a gentle purring sound that calms the Kasanga.

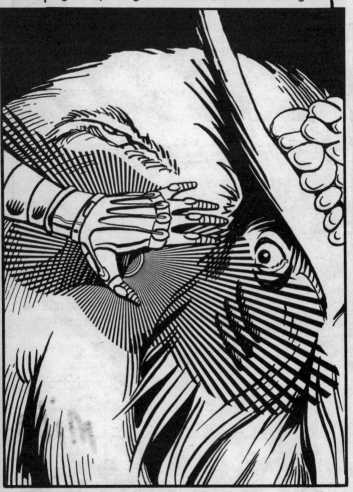

You get closer and see that it has been wounded! Did Marko Khen's agents hurt it when they stole the Kasanga? That would explain why it is ready to attack you. It thinks you have come to take it away!

To look for other clues, turn to page 31.

You find the tank that contains biodroids like the one that helped steal the Kasanga. Your biodroid has already been "picked" as have several others.

You scan the sample of biodroid flesh that you took from the Kasanga's claw. Then your Klagon Hand scans the stems from which the biodroids were detached. The stem that matches your flesh sample is split *evenly*. Which row and column has the *evenly* split stem?

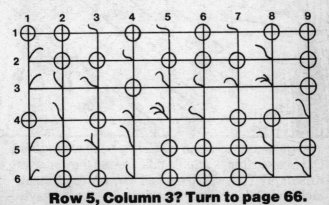

Row 5, Column 3? Turn to page 66.

Row 3, Column 5? Turn to page 22.

You follow the sign to the front of the sub. You go up a flight of stairs to a metal door which slides open as you approach.

You're in the private chamber of Marko Khen, the Galactic Pirate! He laughs cruelly at you and says, "Interplanetary Fools! You have trapped yourselves in my submarine!"

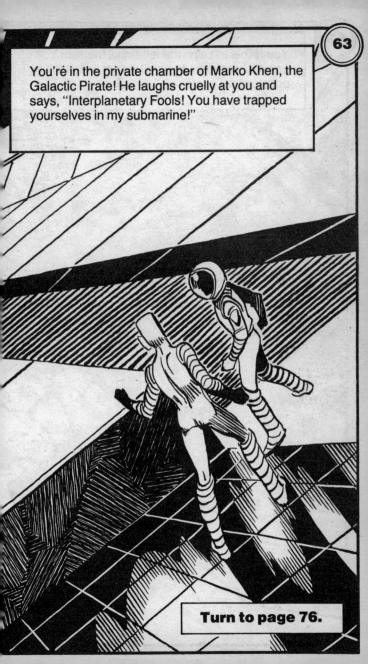

Turn to page 76.

You and the 'droid blast a hole in the portal so that the incoming water will short-circuit the robots and the "electric" mutant Marko.

The Galactic Pirate is stopped in his high-voltage tracks! But you notice that the rest of the glass is starting to crack under the pressure. If too much water pours in, the sub will sink to the bottom of the Frandorian Sea. So will you! **Turn to page 108.**

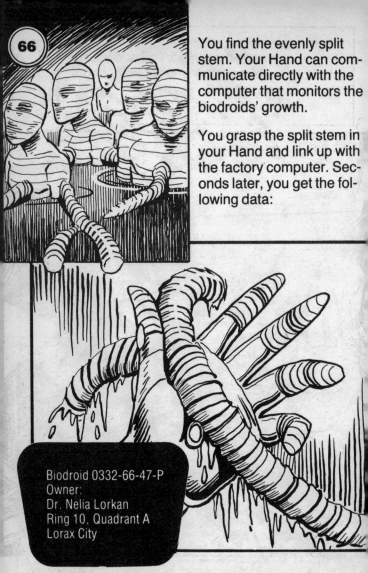

66

You find the evenly split stem. Your Hand can communicate directly with the computer that monitors the biodroids' growth.

You grasp the split stem in your Hand and link up with the factory computer. Seconds later, you get the following data:

Biodroid 0332-66-47-P
Owner:
Dr. Nelia Lorkan
Ring 10, Quadrant A
Lorax City

If the biodroid works for Dr. Nelia Lorkan, then she must be one of Marko Khen's agents. You quickly return to your ship and blast off for Lorax City before the biodroid guards discover you.

Turn to page 84.

As you approach the frigate, you and your biodroid are blasted by a molecular cannon! You crash on the deck.

The End

When you wake up you are a prisoner of the Frandor Buccaneers. You and your biodroid sail the Five Seas of Frandor for the rest of your lives.

You fly up to one of the empty chambers. You see labels for the missing animal in secret code. You can't read it, but it must say Sandragon since you recognize the picture from another mission. You see another code label telling you where the animal has been taken. Using your spy skills, figure out Marko Khen's secret code.

ANIMAL NAME:

| ∽ | = | 7 | 〕 | ⌐ | = | ▷ | ▼ | 7 |

TAKEN TO:

Planet:

| 丫 | ⌐ | = | 7 | 〕 | ▼ | ⌐ |

City:

| 7 | = | 7 | 〕 | ☰ | 7 |

Turn to page 69.

First match Marko's code letters to the letters in Sandragon. Look at the code letters on page 68 that spell out the planet and city that the Sandragon was taken to.

Knowing the letters for S A N D R A G O N, you guess the planet: F R A N D O R.

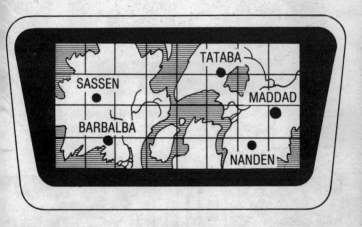

Using the clues on page 68, complete the code chart below.

Now you must go to the city on Frandor where the Sandragon was taken. After you decide which city it is, radio Spy Center and tell them to come to Vantil to pick up the frozen animals and Larat Roz. Then proceed.

Go to Nanden? Turn to page 72.
Go to Sassen? Turn to page 37.

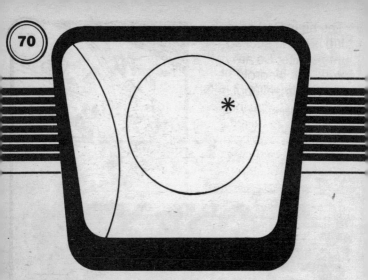

Vantil is marked with an asterisk. Analyzing it with your wrist scanner, you determine that the asterisk indicates the Crystal Caves. Since Dr. Lorkan won't talk, your best lead seems to be to go to the Caves and find out what's there.

You decide to send Dr. Lorkan to Spy Center for questioning. You set her ship's course on autopilot and make sure she can't escape.

Since your own ship has been destroyed, you must fly to Vantil on the back of your biodroid. He is your loyal assistant now. Blast off for Vantil!

Turn to page 88.

The air in Dr. Lorkan's lab is being sucked into space. So are you! The biodroid saves himself, but he can't reach you in time. You're falling. You see a ship below you, the one that blasted your ship. You have a chance to save yourself by grabbing the ship's front section as you fall. But before you reach it, you are blasted by an illusion ray!

You can still see the tail section but not clearly. You must identify the front section through the illusion ray and then grab it!

This shape?
Turn to page 40.

This shape?
Turn to page 79.

72 Your biodroid flies you from Vantil to Nanden, a small port city on Frandor. In the mists, you see a bird—a robot bird! Marko Khen's robot bird must be spying on you. It looks like you picked the right place.

You approach a noisy tavern. Maybe you can get more information if you spy through the window.

Turn to page 73.

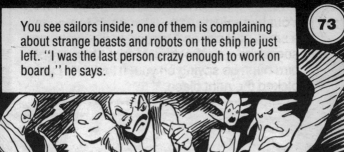

You see sailors inside; one of them is complaining about strange beasts and robots on the ship he just left. "I was the last person crazy enough to work on board," he says.

Now you *know* you are close to Marko Khen! You and your bio-droid fly to the nearby harbor, which is on the Frandorian Sea. You use your Klagon Hand to scan for traces of the stolen animals from the ships leaving the harbor.

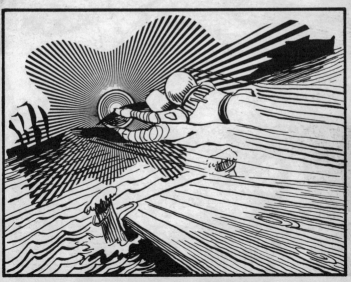

Turn to page 114.

74

You gave the wrong code name! It was not DOMONO! You are arrested. The judge sentences you to 99 years. Before you can give your correct code name, you are sent to hypnoprison. After they get through with you, you don't even remember your real name!

The End

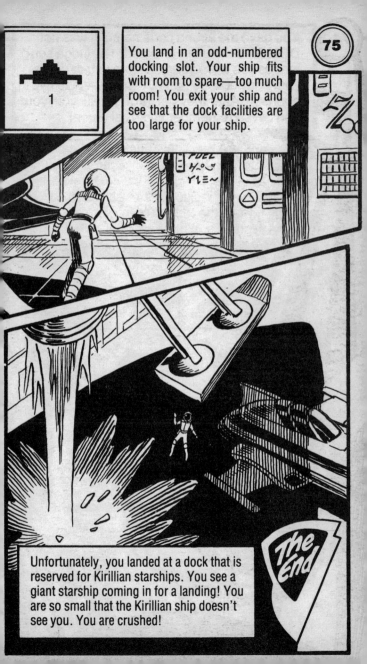

You land in an odd-numbered docking slot. Your ship fits with room to spare—too much room! You exit your ship and see that the dock facilities are too large for your ship.

The End

Unfortunately, you landed at a dock that is reserved for Kirillian starships. You see a giant starship coming in for a landing! You are so small that the Kirillian ship doesn't see you. You are crushed!

You quickly analyze the flight pattern of the robot bird as it flies toward you. Its wings move through four separate positions as it flies. Your wrist scanner tells you that the second position is the robot's most vulnerable point. Blast the robot bird, but be careful! If you make a mistake, the blast will bounce back at you!

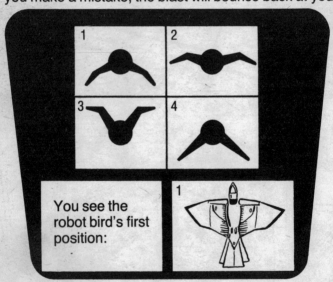

You see the robot bird's first position:

Which will be the robot's second position?

This position? Turn to page 49.

This position? Turn to page 102.

The skin under the Kasanga's claw turns out to be the skin of a biodroid—an artificial human. By analyzing the molecules in the skin, you can trace a biodroid to the factory in which it was manufactured. You link your wrist scanner to your ship's computer files to find out where this biodroid was made.

SCAN RESULTS:

BIODROID: CLASS 47-P
ORIGIN: Factory on Zeta, moon of Frandor, in Sector 5
USES: Laboratory work, bodyguard with visor blast-beam, can fly between planets

You save the skin sample and decide to go to the factory on Zeta. If a biodroid helped steal the Kasangas, its owner must be working for Marko Khen. At the factory you hope to find a clue to the biodroid's owner.

ZZZAAAPPP!

As you leave the area a blast ray shoots past your head!

Turn to page 16.

Good! You land at Ring 10 and dock your ship. You depart and find a sign that reads MUTATION RESEARCH. Dr. Lorkan must be doing mutation research for Marko Khen. You've got to get inside, but the door is locked. You scan the lock with your Klagon Hand. One of your Hand's fingers can match the lock pattern and get you inside.

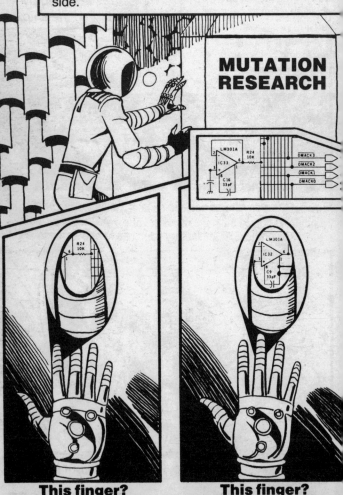

This finger?
Turn to page 117.

This finger?
Turn to page 92.

You did it! Even though you were nearly blinded by the illusion ray, you were able to grab onto the ship.

You pull yourself forward until you reach a window in the front of the ship. You see the ID patch of the owner; it is Dr. Lorkan!

You smash your way into the ship with your Klagon Hand!

Turn to page 56.

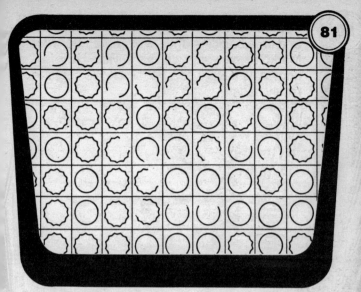

A hatch in the submarine opens, and a herd of robot sea creatures comes out at you. Your wrist scanner shows you that there are two kinds: the deadly Gobblers are *open* on one side. The decoys are *closed* on all sides.

You must melt all the Gobblers together at the same time to stop them. If you hit any of the decoys, they will explode.

Which pattern shows all of the Gobblers and none of the decoys?

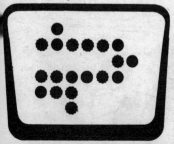

This pattern? Turn to page 94.

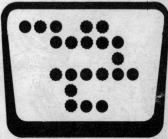

This pattern? Turn to page 90.

You see a herd of animals grazing in the distance. They could be Kasangas.

But to get closer to them, you must pass through the force field. You use your Klagon Hand to search for a gap in the force-field pattern. If you can find one, the Klagon Hand can blast through the force field without setting off an alarm.

Computer Scan: Black shapes are force-field pattern.

Your Klagon Hand has found a flaw in the force field. You'll have to look closely to find the irregular section. Which shape matches the gap in the pattern?

This shape? Turn to page 11. 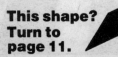 **This shape? Turn to page 35.**

Fire at the force field's weakest spot!

The biodroid is knocked out. You look around the lab. There is no sign of Dr. Lorkan. Then you examine the 'droid and find scars that match the claw patterns of a Kasanga. Dr. Lorkan's biodroid *did* work for Marko Khen. You also see that part of his head seems to be missing.

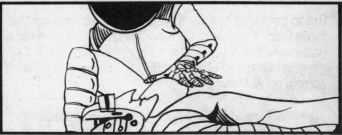

Maybe the biodroid can help you trap Dr. Lorkan. But first you must change the biodroid so that he will be loyal to you. Reprogram the biodroid by firing your laser along the maze of energy channels inside his artificial body. You must pass through his energy nexus or the biodroid may blow up.

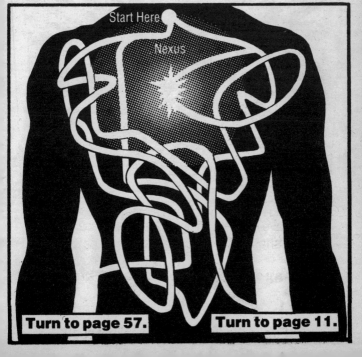

Turn to page 57.   **Turn to page 11.**

You must find Dr. Nelia Lorkan. You have the address (see page 66), but you must figure out the ring and quadrant to land on.

You find Quadrant A easily, but which is the ring that will lead to Dr. Lorkan? When you decide, land your ship there and get out.

Ring X? Turn to page 21.

Ring Y? Turn to page 78.

This biodroid may be faster than you, but you are smarter. You aim for the biodroid's energy nexus—his "heart"—and fire your Klagon Hand's laser.

Your aim is perfect. The biodroid is hit and falls back inside.

Turn to page 83.

They are Kasangas! But as you get close to the herd's leader, it seems ready to attack you.

How could this be? Kasangas are supposed to be peaceful. If this Kasanga starts roaring, the zoo guards will hear it and find you. You decide to use the Klagon Hand's sound device to calm the Kasangas. To activate it, you must speak your code name into the Klagon Hand.

Is your code name DOMINO? Turn to page 60.

Is your code name DOMONO? Turn to page 74.

88 You land on the moon Vantil, at the Crystal Caves. You and your biodroid enter.

The caves reflect images from far away. You see an armed alien. However, you recognize his face from Spy criminal files. <u>It</u> is Larat Roz, one of the few known agents of Marko Khen.

Turn to page 55.

You neutralize the tendrils of the Cranex, but Marko has another trick up his sub!

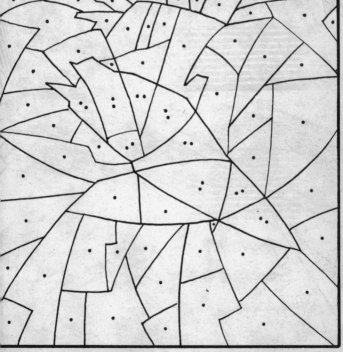

He sends a cloud of dye into the water. You can't see, but you use the Klagon Hand to find Marko's sub by sonar. Look at the glowing surface above. The areas that have *two* dots represent feedback from your sonar. You must fill them in to find the sub.

When you find it, turn to page 118.

Good shooting! You hit all the Gobblers with one blast from your Klagon Hand.

Your shot melts the Gobblers into a a large metal mass. The decoys drift harmlessly to the surface.

Marko Khen will not defeat you that easily!

Turn to page 99.

You reach the grassland zone. The walkways are covered with a force field to protect visitors from the animals, which roam freely. From one walkway, you start looking for the Kasangas.

Turn to page 82.

92 Even spies aren't perfect. You made a mistake. A very bad mistake.

Your protective space suit is blown away!

The End

You and the 'droid track the alien heartbeat to a cavern. You can see Larat Roz through a clear crystal boulder. You must stun him with your Klagon Hand before he sees you. Using the boulder for cover, bounce a shot at a right angle off one of the cavern walls. Only a right-angle shot will connect.

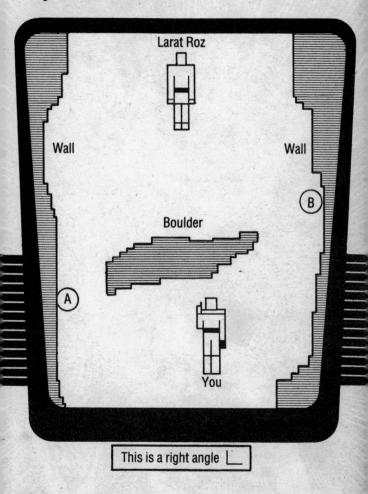

Larat Roz

Wall

Wall

Ⓑ

Boulder

Ⓐ

You

This is a right angle ⌐

Spot A?
Turn to page 80.

Spot B?
Turn to page 51.

94 You blast some of the Gobblers, but your vision is blurred by the sea water. You blast some of the decoys at the same time. The decoys explode! The shock wave from the explosions rocks you.

Before you can use the Klagon Hand again, the unmelted Gobblers attack. They eat the 'droid first, but you're the dessert!

The End

The doors divert the fire.
The animal is knocked out, but Marko is not!

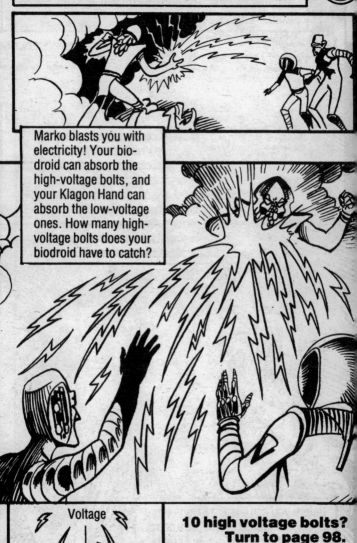

Marko blasts you with electricity! Your bio-droid can absorb the high-voltage bolts, and your Klagon Hand can absorb the low-voltage ones. How many high-voltage bolts does your biodroid have to catch?

Voltage
High | Low

**10 high voltage bolts?
Turn to page 98.**

**12 high voltage bolts?
Turn to page 105.**

Your shot misses. The strange little creature flies around in circles until it zeroes in. Then it blasts you in the back. As you pass out you ask the 'droid to help you, but he does not respond. You'll never know why!

Mutant Marko goes berserk. The mutated animal with him blasts you with fire from its snout. You are able to knock out the animal with your freeze ray, but a stray bolt of electricity has started a fire in the sub!

Your Klagon Hand scans the sub's emergency door-locking system. You can use it to divert the fire away from you. One button can close off the doors that will stop the fire from reaching you.

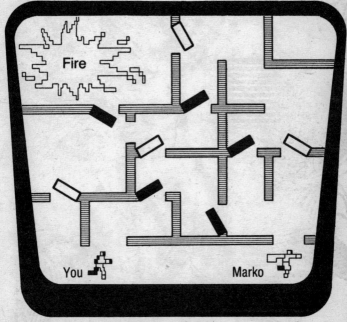

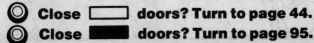

◎ **Close ▭ doors? Turn to page 44.**

◎ **Close ▰ doors? Turn to page 95.**

You made a shocking error! High-voltage electricity runs through your body. There will be Spy-burgers for Marko's mutated monsters tonight!

The End

Fighting the Gobblers has slowed you down. Marko Khen's submarine is getting farther away! You and your biodroid chase the sub past the skeleton of a giant sea monster.

As you catch up, the submarine hatch opens again!

Turn to page 120.

You descend deeper into the tunnel heading left. At the end of the tunnel you find a mutant Zapf! It has three hearts and three heads. Two of the heads want to eat you now, and the majority rules!

The End

Even though Marko is saved and the control room is safely sealed off, nobody is piloting the sub! The robots are all knocked out. Using your wrist scanner, you beam a radio message to your 'droid, who is still in the flooded control room.

101

You order the 'droid to reprogram one of the robot pilots. He opens the robot's brain box. You must tell the 'droid to reactivate the robot's circuits. The 'droid must hit the only buttons that are *touching* with his eye blast. The overlapping buttons are self-destruct circuits!

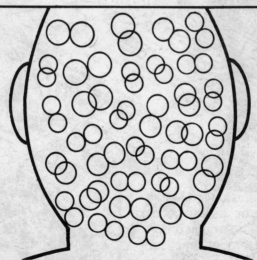

How many buttons are touching? If the 'droid blasts the overlapping ones, the front of the ship will blow up.

32 buttons? Turn to page 104.
40 buttons? Turn to page 92.

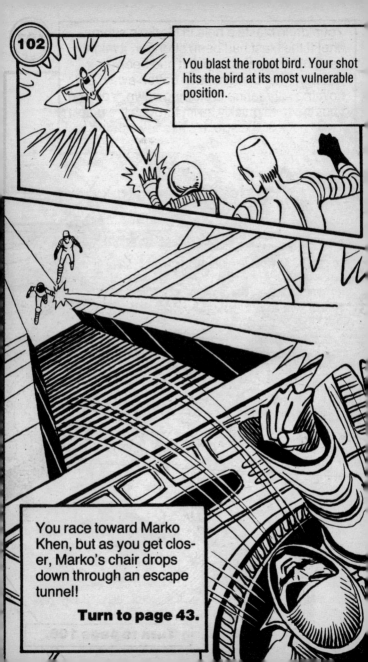

102

You blast the robot bird. Your shot hits the bird at its most vulnerable position.

You race toward Marko Khen, but as you get closer, Marko's chair drops down through an escape tunnel!

Turn to page 43.

Your 'droid blasts a hole in Marko's submarine! If the blast had been stronger, it might have blown up the ship. If it had been weaker, Marko might have gotten away. But now the submarine is slowing down. You and your biodroid quickly swim through the hole in the back of the sub. It's already starting to seal itself!

Turn to page 106.

You did it! The robot is now able to pilot the sub back to the surface. Your biodroid returns with Marko Khen. Rushing back to the mutation chamber, you put the unconscious Pirate and the mutated fire-breathing animal inside and close the door.

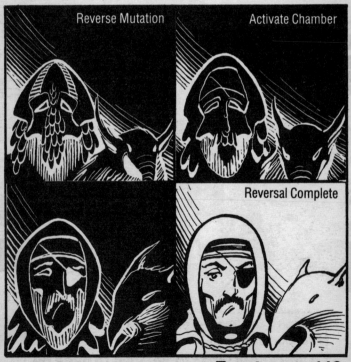

Reverse Mutation

Activate Chamber

Reversal Complete

Turn to page 119.

Your biodroid takes the high volts, and you take the low volts! You chase the mutated Marko past the unconscious animal to the front of the ship. You must catch Marko Khen before he gets to the control room.

Too late! Mutant Marko faces you, protected by his robot crew.

Behind them, a glass portal looks out on the Frandorian Sea.

If you know what to do, turn to page 64.

You slip inside. You head cautiously toward the front of the submarine, on the lookout for Marko's robot bird.

You see two hallways with signs written in Marko's code. (Check page 69 to figure them out.)

You suspect that Marko must be in the front of the ship. You are now in the back. Which corridor will lead you to the front?

Turn to page 62.

Turn to page 39.

You must seal off the portal to stop the flood. You see a control panel nearby, but it is labeled in Marko's secret code. Refer to your data file on page 69, then decode the panel. Which button is most likely to help you in an emergency?

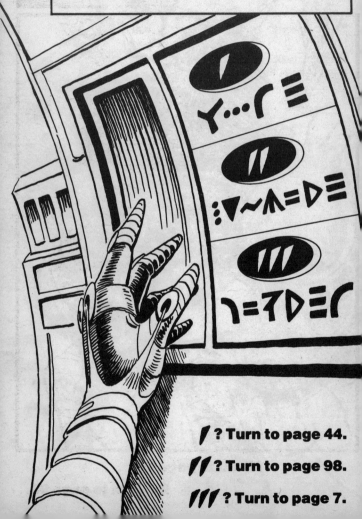

/ ? Turn to page 44.

// ? Turn to page 98.

/// ? Turn to page 7.

A small, strangely familiar-looking creature flies out of the tunnel. Its eye is glowing. It could be coming to rescue Marko Khen!

BLEEP WIR BLEEP

109

You prepare to stun it with your Klagon Hand, but the creature protects itself with ion-gas clouds. How should you aim your Hand to stun the creature's eye?

A

B

A? Turn to page 45.

B? Turn to page 96.

You rush to the glass viewport in the lab's floor to look outside, but before you can get there, the glass is shattered by the force of an explosion. Someone has just blown up your ship!

You should have been more careful. You suspected Marko Khen's agents were on your trail at the zoo!

Turn to page 71.

Even though she is your prisoner, Dr. Lorkan refuses to reveal anything. "Marko Khen has more than enough ways to stop you," she says with a laugh.

"Your biodroid is no longer one of them!" you reply. Dr. Lorkan does not answer. You use your Klagon Hand to probe the ship's computer. You find a map of the Frandor system.

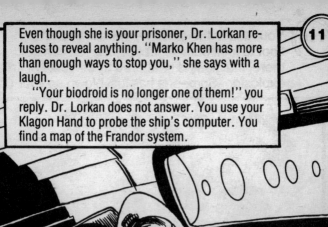

The map is similar to the one you saw on your way to the zoo (see pages 18-19), but is labeled in code. Since each moon is a different size, you can figure out which moon is which. One of the moons is marked with an asterisk.

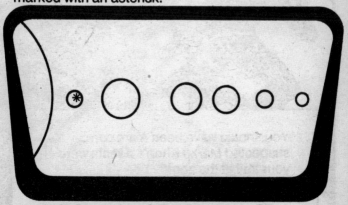

Is it Quondam? Turn to page 37.

Is it Vantil? Turn to page 70.

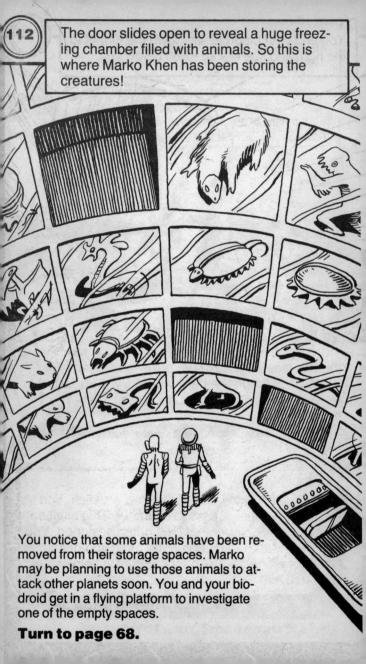

112

The door slides open to reveal a huge freezing chamber filled with animals. So this is where Marko Khen has been storing the creatures!

You notice that some animals have been removed from their storage spaces. Marko may be planning to use those animals to attack other planets soon. You and your bio-droid get in a flying platform to investigate one of the empty spaces.

Turn to page 68.

You and your biodroid slip down the tunnel to the right and see Marko Khen below you.

MUTATION CHAMBER

The Galactic Pirate is about to throw a switch. You see an animal inside a glass chamber. This must be the mutation chamber that Dr. Lorkan designed. You must stop Marko Khen before he turns another animal into a monster. The poor creature is helpless, but you're not!

Turn to page 38.

A sound scan shows you that there are three ships with animals on board. Check your data file on page 26 for the computer codes of animals stolen by Marko Khen. Do any of them match the animals found by your scan?

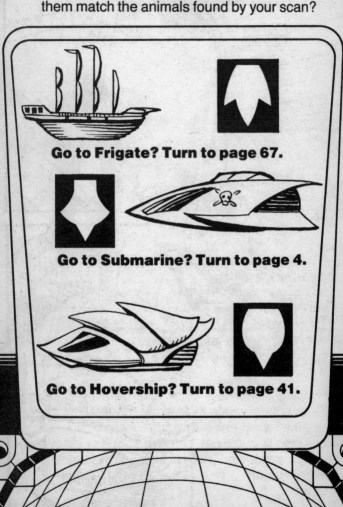

Go to Frigate? Turn to page 67.

Go to Submarine? Turn to page 4.

Go to Hovership? Turn to page 41.

You connect the cables correctly! Your Klagon Hand works! You aim carefully and stun the renegade biodroid with a light blast.

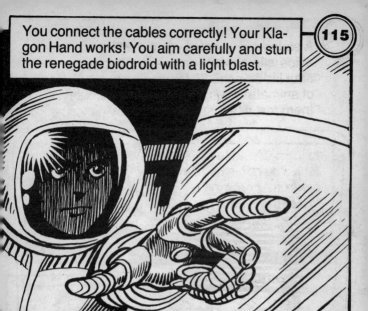

The renegade biodroid will be a danger to you as long as he is controlled by the small part of his head. You must break Marko's control!

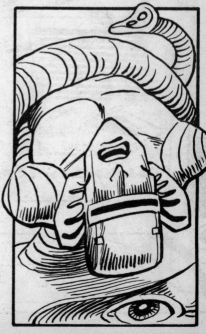

Turn to page 52.

116

You avoid the aster-oids by changing course. You complete your flight to Zeta. You land your ship and walk to the biodroid factory. You can see biodroids "growing" under transparent bubble domes.

You sneak in through a side entrance.

Turn to page 17.

Your Klagon Hand opens the lock instantly.
Now to find Dr. Lorkan!

117

But as the door slides open a biodroid rushes out
and knocks you down. This biodroid has reflexes
faster than a human being's. You must act quickly.

Turn to page 86.

118 You've found the sub. Marko's on the run, but you're close enough for the biodroid to eye blast the submarine to slow it down. He can shoot farther than your Hand, but needs to know how much energy to use. Figure out exactly how far the sub is from you.

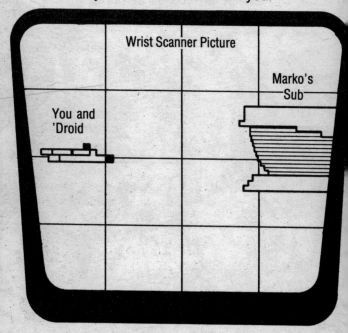

Wrist Scanner Picture

Marko's Sub

You and 'Droid

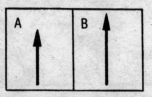

Power Available

A ↑   B ↑

Energy Readout (½ Size of Scanner Picture)

Arrow A? Turn to page 49.
Arrow B? Turn to page 103.

You've captured Marko Khen, the Galactic Pirate! Now to complete your mission. You make him take you and the biodroid to a room where he's keeping the rest of the stolen animals. The Kasanga is there; so is the missing Sandragon. You notify Interplanetary Spy Center that you will be bringing them back safe and sound!

119

Turn to page 121.

A bizarre, gigantic creature comes out of Marko's submarine. This time it's one of Marko's mutated animals! You use your Klagon Hand to find out that the creature was once a peaceful water creature known as a Cranex.

CRANEX (Normal)

Marko has turned the innocent Cranex into a monster! The mutant Cranex has long tendrils that explode when two of them touch.

Turn to page 42.

As the sub reaches the surface of the Frandorian Sea, you launch it out of the water and into space! Your first stop will be the Interplanetary Zoo, to return the animals. Then you will take Marko Khen to the Alvarian Police.

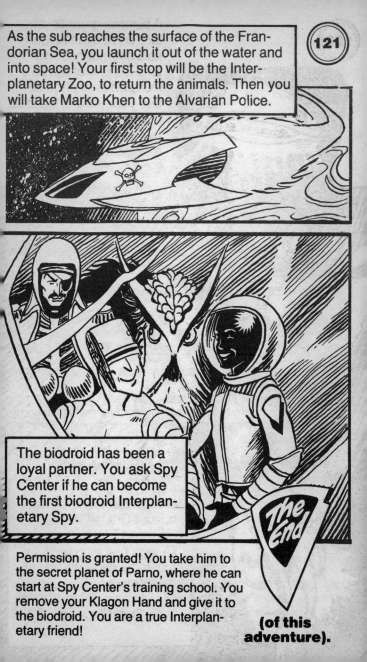

The biodroid has been a loyal partner. You ask Spy Center if he can become the first biodroid Interplanetary Spy.

The End

Permission is granted! You take him to the secret planet of Parno, where he can start at Spy Center's training school. You remove your Klagon Hand and give it to the biodroid. You are a true Interplanetary friend!

(of this adventure).

If you enjoyed this book, you can look forward to these other **Be An Interplanetary Spy** books:

#1 FIND THE KIRILLIAN! by McEvoy, Hempel and Wheatley

The ruthless interplanetary criminal Phatax has kidnapped Prince Quizon of Alvare, guardian of the Royal Jewels. You must journey to the planet Threefax, find the Prince and capture Phatax!

#2 THE GALACTIC PIRATE by McEvoy, Hempel and Wheatley

Marko Khen, the Galactic Pirate, has been using his band of criminals to kidnap rare animals from the Interplanetary Zoo. You must find Marko Khen and prevent him from changing the animals into monsters!

#3 ROBOT WORLD by McEvoy, Hempel and Wheatley

Dr. Cyberg, the computer genius, has designed a planet of robots to help humanity. But the robots rebel and Dr. Cyberg disappears! You must track down Dr. Cyberg and face one of the most incredible starships in the galaxy!

#4 SPACE OLYMPICS by Martinez and Pierard

The insidious Gresh, master spy, has threatened to sabotage the galaxy's most famous sports event. You must protect the star of the planet Nez, the super-athlete Andromeda, as she makes her way through the games of the Space Olympics!